Amelia
Gets Into Trouble!

Enid Blyton™

Amelia Jane Gets Into Trouble!

EGMONT

EGMONT

We bring stories to life

First published in Great Britain 1954 by Newnes
as part of *More About Amelia Jane!*
Reissued 2014 by Dean,
an imprint of Egmont UK Limited
The Yellow Building, 1 Nicholas Road, London W11 4AN

Text copyright © 1954 Hodder & Stoughton Ltd
Illustration copyright © 2001 Hodder & Stoughton Ltd

ENID BLYTON ® Copyright © 2014 Hodder & Stoughton Ltd

ISBN 978 0 6035 7028 5
58469/1

A CIP catalogue record for this title is available from the British Library

Typeset by Dorchester Typesetting Group Ltd
Printed and bound in Great Britain by the CPI Group

Contents

Amelia Jane and the Telephone

There was a new toy in the nursery. It was a little telephone. It stood on the nursery book-shelf looking exactly like a real one, but much smaller.

The toys didn't dare to touch it. They were afraid of the real telephone, and they were afraid of the toy one, too.

Outside in the passage they often heard the bell of the real telephone ringing loudly, and it made them jump. Then someone would come along, take the receiver off the telephone and speak into it.

'Hallo!' they would say. 'Hallo!' And then they would speak to somebody far, far away, and it all seemed very like magic.

Amelia Jane, the big naughty doll, had been away for a few days. When she came back the first thing she saw was the toy telephone.

'Aha!' she said, and went over to it. 'A telephone. Good. We need one in the nursery.'

'Don't touch it, Amelia Jane – a telephone is very magic,' cried Tom the toy soldier. 'Voices come into it, you know – people who are far, far away can speak to you. Be careful, in case somebody's voice is in that toy telephone now!'

'Pooh!' said Amelia Jane. 'I'm just going to do a bit of ordering – like Mother does sometimes on the real telephone out in the passage.'

And, to the toys' horror, she picked up the little receiver, put one end to her ear, and spoke into the other end.

'Is that the butcher? Send four sausages to the nursery, please. Is that the baker? Send four buns to the nursery, please. Is that the watchmaker? Send one nice new watch to the nursery, please – and, oh, please see that the letters

A. J. are on the back. A. J. for Amelia Jane. Thank you.' She put back the receiver and smiled round at the astonished toys. 'There you are! I've done a nice little bit of ordering. We'll enjoy the sausages and the buns. We can divide them up between us. And I always wanted a watch.'

Of course, Amelia Jane knew quite well that she hadn't been speaking to the butcher, the baker and the watchmaker. She was just making the toys think she was very daring and grand.

But the toys were really very worried. They climbed up to the window-sill to watch for the goods to arrive.

'The thing is – how are we to pay for them?' said the teddy bear. 'I haven't got any money!'

'I've got a penny that I found under the carpet,' said the clockwork mouse.

'Shall we be put into prison if we order things we can't pay for?' asked the clockwork clown.

Nobody knew – but they thought it was very likely. Tom the toy soldier went to Amelia Jane.

'Please, Amelia Jane, ring up the butcher, the baker and the watchmaker and tell them not to send the things after all,' he said.

'What will you give me if I do?' asked Amelia Jane at once.

'Oh dear – I'll give you my best hanky,' said Tom. 'And the mouse will give you his penny. Have *you* got anything to give, Teddy?'

'Just a good scolding,' said the
teddy, rather fiercely. 'I'll give that
with pleasure.'

'Give me the hanky and the
money, and I'll ring up the butcher,
the baker and the watchmaker,' said
Amelia Jane. So they gave her them,
and she went to the telephone.

'I haven't given you my scolding,'
said the bear, but Amelia took no
notice. She spoke into the telephone:

'Is that the butcher? We don't want
the sausages after all. Is that the
baker? We don't want the buns. Is that
the watchmaker? I've changed my
mind about the watch. Yes – yes.
That's right. What's that? You want
to send a message to the teddy bear?
Oh, yes, of course, I'll give it to him.'

The toys were listening with all

their ears. 'Right,' said Amelia, into the telephone. 'I'm to tell the bear he is a nasty, fat, tubby little creature, who can't even growl like a bear. Yes, certainly I'll tell him!'

'Don't you dare to tell me,' said the bear fiercely.

'All right, Teddy, I won't tell you that you are a nasty, fat, tubby little creature who can't even growl like a bear,' said Amelia Jane, annoyingly.

'But you *have* told him!' said Tom.

'No – I just told him what I wouldn't tell him,' said Amelia Jane.

She climbed up on to a shelf where nobody could reach her, not even the bear. She thought about the toy telephone. It would be very very useful, she could see that. She would be able to make up all kinds of rude messages to pass on to the toys. She began to make a little plan.

Yes – she would invent somebody at the other end – somebody who would keep ringing up – and she would pretend to answer the telephone, and then give the horrid messages to all the toys. That would keep them in order all right!

She slipped down and went to the small toy bicycle that stood at one end of the nursery. It had a tiny little bell. She unscrewed it and put it into her pocket. She could ring it whenever she wanted to – and she would pretend it was the telephone bell ringing. That would make the toys jump!

The toys made up a song about Amelia Jane.

Amelia Jane
Is naughty again,
Let's go and leave her
Out in the rain.
Nobody loves her,
Nobody cares
If she gets eaten
By lions or bears.
She wants a scolding,
It's perfectly plain;
Amelia Jane,
You are naughty again!

Amelia listened to this song and felt very angry indeed. How dare they sing that? Why, even the clockwork mouse was singing and waving his tail about in time to the tune. Amelia walked over to the telephone and sat down by it.

She put her hand into her pocket and rang the little bell. It sounded just like the telephone bell suddenly ringing. The toys stopped singing in great surprise.

'The telephone rang!' they said to one another. 'Would you believe it? The telephone rang. Answer it, Amelia. See who wants to speak to us.'

Amelia picked up the receiver and put one end to her ear. 'Dear me – is that really Mr Mumbo-Jumbo?' she said, sounding astonished. 'This is Amelia Jane. What do you want, dear Mr Mumbo-Jumbo?'

The toys listened to this in amazement. Amelia Jane went on speaking. 'Yes, yes – I'll tell the bear. You're coming for him this evening, and you'll pull his nose for him till it's as long as an elephant's trunk. Yes, Mr Mumbo-Jumbo. Oh, yes – he is a bad bear. He deserves it. I'm sorry he was once so rude to you. Goodbye.'

She put down the receiver. The bear was trembling like a jelly, he was so scared.

'I was never rude to Mr Mumbo-Jumbo,' he wailed. 'I don't even know him. I never met him. I won't have my nose pulled, I won't, I won't.'

'I won't let you,' said Tom, comfortingly. 'I'll fight him.'

'So will I,' said the clockwork mouse, bravely. 'I'll nibble a hole in his leg.'

The telephone bell rang again –
though, of course, it was only Amelia
Jane putting her hand into her pocket
and ringing the little bicycle bell. She
picked up the receiver again and
spoke into it.

'Hallo! Who's that? Oh, Mr
Mumbo-Jumbo again – what do you
want this time, dear Mr Mumbo-

Jumbo? Yes, the clockwork mouse lives here – and the toy soldier too. No, they are not very nice toys. What am I to tell them? You are coming tonight to catch the toy soldier and peg him to your clothes-line? And you're going to peg the clockwork mouse up by his tail? Right, I'll tell them. Goodbye.'

'Oooooh!' squealed the clockwork mouse in fright. 'He's not to come! I never did him any harm!'

'Nor did I,' said Tom, turning pale. 'Who's this awful fellow? He's not to come. I've never been pegged up on a clothes-line in my life, and nobody's going to do that to me.'

The bell rang again and Amelia Jane once more spoke into the telephone. 'Oh – it's you, Mr Mumbo-Jumbo, again. What's that?

You'll scold any toy who is rude to me? Thank you very much indeed. I'll tell you tonight who you can scold very severely!'

She made a rude face at the listening toys and went over to her cot. She climbed in. 'I'm going to have a good sleep,' she said. 'And anyone who disturbs me will be reported to Mr Mumbo-Jumbo!'

She shut her eyes and was soon fast asleep. She turned in her sleep – and out of her pocket fell the little bicycle bell!

The clockwork clown pounced on it.

'Look at that! She rang this when she wanted us to think it was the telephone ringing! It was all a pretence on her part, the wicked doll.

There wasn't any Mr Mumbo-Jumbo speaking to her over the telephone!'

'Let's wake her,' said Tom fiercely.

'No,' said the clown, speaking in a whisper. 'I've got a better idea. I know where there's a long piece of rubber tubing. I'll get it and fix it to the ear-piece of the telephone – and then, whoever speaks at the other end of the rubber tube can be heard in the telephone – *really* heard, not just pretending.'

'What's the use of that?' asked the bear.

'Wait and see,' said the clown. 'Now tonight one of us will ring this little bell, as if the telephone was ringing again – and Amelia can go and answer it – and Tom shall speak through the tube . . .'

'Oooooh, yes,' said everyone. 'That's a fine idea!'

'And he shall say, in a very dreadful voice: "This is Mr Mumbo-Jumbo speaking. Is that Amelia Jane? I've heard what a bad doll you are. And I'm coming to get you, Amelia. I'm walking up the passage now – I'm banging at the door. Let me in!"'

'But – what's the good of that?' said the bear. 'He won't come walking up and banging at the door.'

'Yes, he will,' grinned the clown. 'I shall be outside, listening – and *I'll* come stamping up the passage, and *I'll* bang hard at the door – see?'

'Amelia will think it's really Mr Mumbo-Jumbo out there and she'll be scared out of her life!' said the bear, chuckling. 'What a fine idea. Where's the rubber tube, clown?'

Well, before Amelia woke up, the rubber tubing was fixed to the telephone and run secretly into the toy-cupboard, where Tom was hiding. They all waited till Amelia awoke and stepped out of the cot.

At the same moment the bear, who was by the telephone, rang the little bell that had fallen from Amelia's pocket. 'R-r-r-r-ring!'

Amelia jumped and looked surprised. But she walked over to the telephone and took off the receiver, meaning to make up some more messages from Mumbo-Jumbo. But to her astonishment and horror, a deep, hollow voice came to her ear.

'Is that Amelia Jane? This is Mr Mumbo-Jumbo speaking. I've heard what a bad doll you are. And I'm coming to get you, Amelia. I'm walking up the passage now – I'm BANGING at the door. Let me in!'

Amelia listened in fright. There really *was* somebody speaking through the telephone this time – somebody who said he was *Mr Mumbo-Jumbo*!

Then she heard the footsteps stamping up the passage outside, where the clown had hidden himself. She heard the loud banging at the door, and the shouts of 'Let me in!'

'No, no – don't let him in!' she wailed, and she ran to the toy-cupboard. 'Don't open the door, toys. I'll be good. I'll never be bad again. I'll give you back your hanky, Tom, and your money, Mouse. Oh, oh, don't let Mr Mumbo-Jumbo in.'

Bang-bang-BANG! 'Let me in,
I say!'

Amelia piled bricks all over herself
in the cupboard, trying to hide. Tom
went to the door of the nursery and
spoke sternly through it.

'Go away, Mr Mumbo-Jumbo.
We will let you know if Amelia Jane is
naughty again, and you can come
and get her then.'

And to Amelia's great relief she

heard footsteps stamping away from the door, and the banging stopped.

'Well, we've saved you from your friend, Mr Mumbo-Jumbo,' said Tom, looking into the cupboard. 'Are you going to behave yourself now, or not?'

'Oh, yes, yes,' sobbed Amelia Jane. 'Oh, that awful toy telephone. I'll never use it again.'

She didn't, of course. And, strange to say, neither did Mr Mumbo-Jumbo!

Now Then, Amelia Jane!

Amelia Jane, the big naughty doll in the nursery, was doing a bit of sewing. She sat in the corner, her head bent over her work, sewing away.

'Aha! So you've decided to sew on that shoe button at last!' said the clockwork clown, coming up. 'Quite time, too – your shoe's fallen off heaps of times!'

'You be quiet,' said Amelia Jane.

'And while you're about it, why not mend that hole in your dress?' said a wooden skittle, hopping up. 'Or do you *like* holes in your dress, Amelia Jane?'

'You be quiet, too,' said Amelia, and jabbed at him with her needle. He

hopped away with a chuckle.

He was soon back again. 'And what about your right stocking?' he said. 'It's got a great big hole in the heel. And what about . . . ?'

Amelia Jane jabbed at him again so hard that the thimble flew off her finger. It rolled away over the floor into a corner.

'Bother you, skittle!' said Amelia Jane, in a temper. 'Now you go and pick up that thimble and bring it back to me! Why do you tease me like this? I don't like you.'

'Shan't pick up your thimble!' said the skittle, enjoying himself. 'Silly old Amelia Jane!'

'Stop yelling at one another, and you go and pick up the thimble, skittle,' said the teddy bear, crossly.

'Can't you see I'm trying to read?'

The skittle didn't dare to disobey the big fat bear. He had once been rude to the bear and the bear had sat on him for a whole day, and the skittle hadn't liked that at all. The bear was so heavy.

So he picked up the thimble – but he didn't give it back to Amelia Jane. No – he put it on his head for a hat! Then he walked up and down in a very silly way, saying, 'Look at my new hat! Oh, *do* look at my new hat!'

Everybody looked, of course, and all the toys laughed at the skittle because he really did look funny in a thimble-hat.

He took it off and bowed to them, and then put it back again.

'*Will* you give me my thimble?' cried Amelia Jane, in a rage. 'Give it to me AT ONCE!'

'Say "please", Amelia,' said the bear. 'You sound very rude.'

'I *shan't* say "please"!' cried Amelia. 'And don't you interfere. Skittle, if you don't give me back my thimble at once I'll chase you and knock you over!'

'Can't catch *me*! Can't catch *me*!' said the skittle, who was really being very funny and very annoying. He ran here and there, and he kept taking his thimble-hat on and off to Amelia in a very ridiculous way.

Well, Amelia Jane wasn't going to

let a skittle be cheeky to her, so up she
got. She raced after the skittle, and he
rushed away. But Amelia Jane caught
him – and do you know what she did?
Instead of taking the thimble off his
head, she pushed it so hard that it
went right over the poor skittle's nose,
and he couldn't see a thing.

'Oh! Oh, it's so tight now I can't
get it off!' yelled the skittle, trying to

force the thimble off his head.

Amelia Jane laughed.

'That'll teach you to wear my thimble for a hat and be so rude to me,' she said.

'Help, help!' shouted the skittle. 'It's hurting me! Oooooooooh! Ow! OOOOOOOOOOOH!'

'It really *is* hurting him,' said the bear, getting up. 'Dear, dear – I shall never finish my book today. Stand still, you silly skittle. I'll take the thimble off.'

Well, he tugged and he pulled, and he pulled and he tugged – but he couldn't get that thimble off!

Then Tom the toy soldier came up and had a try – but he couldn't get the thimble off either.

Amelia Jane tried – but it wasn't a

bit of good; that thimble was jammed so hard on the skittle's head that it really could *not* be moved!

'You'll have to wear the thimble always,' said the bear at last. The skittle lay down and yelled.

'I can't! I don't want to! Take it off, take it off! It's tight, I tell you!'

'We'll simply *have* to do something,' said Tom. 'Else the skittle will go on yelling for ever, and I don't think I could bear that.'

'Of *course* something must be done,' said the other skittles, who had popped up, looking very worried. 'Amelia Jane is very naughty.'

'That's nothing new,' said the bear. 'Dear me, do stop yelling, skittle. You'll wake up the household!'

Then the bear thought of

something. 'Oh, I've got an idea,' he said. 'What about going out to ask the little pixie who lives in the pansy bed if he knows of a spell to help us. A Get-Loose Spell, perhaps.'

'A good idea,' said Tom. 'Amelia Jane, go and find the pixie and ask him.'

'What! In the middle of a dark night!' said Amelia Jane. 'No, thank you. And anyway, I don't like that pixie!'

'Amelia Jane, if you don't go and ask him, we shall take your best ribbon and hide it,' said the bear.

'Oh, no, don't do that!' said Amelia. 'It's my party ribbon. All right, you horrid things – I'll go. But I know a very good way of getting the thimble off the skittle.'

'How?' asked the toys.

'Chop off his head!' said Amelia Jane. 'He has so few brains that he'd never even notice his head was gone!'

'We *will* take away your best ribbon now,' said the bear, as the skittle gave a loud yell of fright.

'No, no – I didn't mean it!' said Amelia Jane. 'I'll go this very minute to find the pixie.'

Well, off she went, climbing out of the window and down to the pansy bed.

The little pixie was there, wide awake.

'Pixie,' began Amelia, 'I want your help.'

'What will you give me for it?' asked the pixie, at once. He didn't like Amelia.

'Nothing,' said Amelia. 'Oh – let go of my foot, you horrid little pixie!'

'I'm taking your shoe for payment,' said the pixie. 'And the other one too. They will fit me nicely. Now, it's no good yelling. I've got them. I've no doubt you've been just as naughty as usual, so it serves you right. Now – what do you want my help for?'

Amelia Jane told him sulkily. 'The skittle is wearing my thimble jammed down hard on his head. How can we get it off?'

'Make the thimble bigger, of course,' said the pixie. 'Then his head will be too small for it and it will slip off.'

'But how can we make the thimble bigger?' asked Amelia Jane.

'Easy,' said the pixie. 'If you heat anything made of metal it becomes just a tiny bit larger – so heat the thimble, Amelia – and it will slip off the skittle's head.'

'But how can we heat it?' said Amelia, not really believing the pixie.

'Stand him on his head in hot water,' said the pixie. 'You could have thought of that yourself. Now go away. I want to try on your shoes.'

Amelia went back to the nursery. 'The pixie says that if we stand the skittle on his head in hot water, the thimble will get a bit larger and slip off,' said Amelia.

'I don't believe a word of it,' said the bear.

'Well, that's what he *said*,' said Amelia. 'He didn't tell me anything else. And I had to give him my shoes for that advice.'

'Hm,' said Tom. 'Well, poor old skittle – we'd better try it, anyway. Bear, put a little hot water into the basin, will you? Don't put the plug in in case it gets too deep – just let the water run in and out, and we'll pop the skittle in on his head, and heat the thimble in the water.'

Well, the skittle howled and yelled and kicked up a great fuss, but the bear and the toy soldier were very

 firm with him. They turned him upside down and held him in the hot water, so that the heat

warmed up the thimble on his head.

And will you believe it? – the
thimble slipped off, just as the pixie
had said it would. But alas – it rolled
round the basin, and disappeared
down the plughole! It was gone!

'Oh – my thimble, my thimble!'
yelled Amelia Jane. But it was gone
for good. Nobody ever saw it again.

'Serves you right, Amelia,' said the
bear, turning the poor skittle the right
way up again. 'Well, who would have
thought the pixie knew a spell like
that? Did *you* know that heat made
things just a bit bigger, clockwork
clown?'

'I never did,' said the clown.

But the funny thing is that it's *true*!
So if ever a thimble gets stuck on one
of your skittles you'll know what to do

– stand him on his head in hot water
and it will slip off!

And now Amelia Jane can't *bear*
doing her mending, because she
hasn't got a thimble and she pricks
her finger all the time. Still, as the
toys tell her – it's her own fault!

Amelia Jane Gets Into Trouble

Amelia Jane, as you all know, is a very clever and very naughty doll. The toys could never keep pace with her tricks – but one day she got herself into trouble.

It happened like this. Billy came into the nursery and looked round for his soldier doll. 'Tom, where are you?' he said. 'I'm going to take you to tea with me this afternoon and I'm going

in *my* soldier things, too! We're going
to play with Betty and Dick, and
they're going to dress up as soldiers as
well. So, with you, we'll be four
soldiers! We'll have fun!'

He began looking for Tom, the
soldier. But before he could find him
his mother called out. 'Billy! Come
here a minute. I want you.'

Billy ran out. Amelia Jane sat up,
her eyes gleaming. 'Tom, don't you
go! They'll do
awful things to
you!'

'Oh
dear!' said
Tom, in
alarm.
Although
he was a

soldier doll, he wasn't at all brave really. 'Oh dear! I don't want to go. I really don't!'

'Well, I'll go instead,' said Amelia Jane, in a kind voice. 'I'll do you a good turn and put on your clothes and go instead of you. Would you like that?'

'Oh, yes!' said Tom. He stripped off his soldier clothes, and Amelia Jane dressed herself up in them. My word, she did look different. You should have seen her! She pranced about looking very smart in Tom's trousers and jacket. 'I'm grand! I'm brave!'

She began to rush at the toys, pretending to capture them. They didn't like it at all.

'Now stop that, Amelia Jane!' said the sailor doll. 'And take off those clothes. You know perfectly well that nobody will harm Tom if he goes out to tea – you've only said that because you want to dress up and prance about pretending to be a soldier. Take those clothes off.'

But all that Amelia Jane did was to rush at the toy clown and the sailor doll, and pretend to capture them. They were very cross indeed – but Amelia was bigger than they were, and it was difficult to stop her.

In rushed Billy. He caught hold of Amelia Jane, thinking she was Tom, his soldier doll. Out of the door he went at top speed, calling out, 'I'm ready, Mother! I'm just coming!'

Amelia Jane planned to have a wonderful time. She would go stalking Betty and Dick with Billy. She would take them prisoner. My goodness, Amelia Jane was going to have the time of her life!

But it didn't turn out quite like that. Billy, Betty and Dick got the gardener to hide Amelia Jane somewhere, so that they could stalk her and pounce on her and take her prisoner!

So Amelia was put into the middle of a bush by the gardener, and left there. The children began to hunt for her, going along in single file, leaping high in the air, and filling the garden with loud cries.

Amelia Jane shivered in the bush. How she hoped they wouldn't find her. She didn't mind stalking the others and pouncing on them – but she didn't want to be pounced on and taken prisoner herself!

Well, the children soon found her. They surrounded the bush, and Betty yelled out loudly: 'The enemy is hiding here! I see him! Come on, soldiers, come on!'

And they all pounced! Amelia Jane was pulled roughly from the bush and thrown to the ground.

'You're our prisoner!' yelled the three, and ran round her. They didn't even touch Amelia, but she thought they were going to every time they came.

'Let's tie him to a tree,' said Billy. So they took Amelia and tied her to a little tree.

'Funny sort of doll, this,' said
Dick, looking closely at her. 'He's got
a face more like a girl-doll than a
boy-doll.'

'Now he's tied up. He can't get
away. He's our prisoner,' said Betty.

But fortunately for Amelia Jane,
the tea-bell rang loudly, and the three
soldiers raced up to the house in glee.

Amelia Jane began to sob. She
struggled with the knots that tied her,
but they were tight and she couldn't
undo even one of them. She was very
frightened. How she wished she
hadn't been silly enough to make
Tom give her his clothes!

'I'm always doing silly things!'
wept Amelia. 'I wish I didn't. Oh,
what shall I do?'

She waited for the children to

come back. She waited and she waited. But they didn't come. Betty's mother had said she thought it was going to rain, so they could either play a *quiet* game of soldiers indoors, or a noisy game of snap, whichever they liked.

They chose snap, and forgot all about Amelia Jane, tied to the tree in the garden. In fact Billy forgot about her completely, and even went home without her! So there she was when darkness came, still tied up tightly, jumping in fright every time an owl came by and hooted.

The toys were surprised when Billy came home without Amelia Jane. He didn't say anything about leaving her behind until just before he went to bed. He was sitting in his pyjamas eating his supper in the nursery with his sister, when he suddenly gave a cry.

'What's the matter?' said his mother.

'It's Tom. I've forgotten to bring him home,' said Billy. 'We tied him up to a tree and then we went in to tea and I forgot all about him. He's still there, poor thing. And it's dark and rainy. Mother, I must go and get him.'

'No, you mustn't,' said his mother, firmly. 'You are certainly not going to run down the dark rainy street in your pyjamas. You can get Tom tomorrow. If he's under a tree he won't get very wet.'

'But he'll be frightened,' said Billy. 'He won't like it.'

'Well, that's your fault,' said his mother. 'When we forget things we often make others suffer as well as ourselves. You should have remembered to bring Tom home.'

Now, of course, the toys couldn't help hearing all this, because they were sitting round the nursery watching the children eat their supper. They were full of horror.

What! Amelia Jane tied up to a tree, left alone in the darkness and the rain! Naughty as she was, and cross as they felt with her, they were very sorry. When the children had gone to bed they got together in a corner and talked about it.

'I'll go and rescue her,' said Tom, bravely. 'I know the way. I've been to that house before.'

'But you haven't got any clothes on,' said the sailor doll. 'You'll get soaked. And it's frightening to go out in the dark at night. You might meet a fierce dog or a yowling cat who would pounce on you. Anyway, you're not very brave.'

'Oh, I know that,' said Tom, sadly. 'It's a pity to have to be a soldier doll and not feel brave. That's really why I'm going. I'm not brave, in fact I'm very frightened, but I feel I *ought* to be brave, so I'm going to rescue Amelia.'

'Well, that's very nice of you, after she tricked you into taking off your clothes and letting her go out to tea instead of you,' said the toy clown, patting Tom on the back. 'All right, you go then, if you know the way. What about clothes? There's a little

cape and hat in the doll's wardrobe.
You could borrow those.'

So Tom put them on and he looked
rather odd, not at all like a soldier
doll! Then he slipped out of the
window, climbed down the tree
outside and set off in the darkness to
Betty's house.

The rain hit him on the nose, and
ran down his cloak in little rivers. It
went down his neck too, because his
hat didn't fit very well. At last he
came to the garden of Betty's house
and slipped through a hole in the
fence.

Amelia Jane was still tied to the
tree. An owl had hooted in her ear. A
spider had walked over her face. A
hedgehog had walked so near that his
spines pricked her legs. She was lonely

and scared.

She heard a noise. What was that? Oh, what was that? It sounded like someone coming nearer and nearer, creeping through the bushes! Amelia began to tremble and shake.

'Who is it? Go away! Leave me alone! Oh, don't come near me, I'm scared, I'm frightened! Don't frighten me any more. Go away, whoever it is!'

But the footsteps came nearer and nearer, and then a head poked round a bush. Amelia Jane gave a scream.

'Go away! I'm frightened of you!'

Well it was Tom, of course, come to rescue her! 'It's all right,' he said. 'It's only me, Tom. I'll undo your knots, Amelia Jane.'

Amelia could have hugged him!

Dear, dear Tom! Oh, how could she have tricked him like that! She would always, always love him now.

He undid the knots. She stretched herself stiffly and then sneezed. 'Let's hurry home,' said Tom. 'You've caught a cold. I'll lead the way.'

Well, it wasn't long before they were both back in the nursery again, leaving little wet marks all over the floor. As soon as they got there Amelia Jane flung herself on Tom and hugged him so hard that he squealed.

'Good, kind, *brave* Tom! Oh, what courage you've got! Oh, how plucky you are! Toys, Tom is quite the bravest toy in the nursery!'

Tom could hardly believe his ears when all the toys crowded round and thumped him on the back, and said the same as Amelia! 'But I'm not brave!' he kept saying. 'I never have been! I was frightened all the time. Brave people aren't frightened.'

'The bravest people of all are those who are frightened and yet go on being brave,' said the sailor doll, helping him off with his wet cloak. 'Amelia Jane has no right to wear a soldier's clothes – she's a little coward! As soon as they are dry, you must wear them again, because you really and truly are a brave soldier!'

The toys dried Tom's clothes, as soon as Amelia Jane had taken them off. Amelia dressed humbly in her own clothes. She felt ashamed of herself. She sneezed loudly.

'I'm getting a dreadful cold,' she said, very sorry for herself.

'It serves you right,' said the sailor doll. 'Don't sneeze all over us, please. We're giving a party for Tom soon, and you'd better not come in case you give everyone your cold.'

So now Amelia Jane is sitting by herself in a corner sneezing into her hanky, watching the most wonderful party going on, given for Tom, the soldier doll. Nobody feels at all sorry for her. I don't know if you do?

Billy's going to be very surprised tomorrow to find that Tom is sitting in the nursery instead of tied up to the tree! He's going to puzzle about that for days.

Amelia Jane Has a Good Idea

The new teddy bear was very small indeed. The toys stared at him when he first came into the playroom, wondering what he was.

'Good gracious! I believe you're a teddy bear!' said Amelia Jane, the big, naughty doll. 'I thought you were a peculiar-shaped mouse.'

'Well, I'm not,' said the small bear, sharply, and pressed himself in the

middle. 'Grrrrrr! Hear
me growl? Well, no
mouse can growl. It
can only squeak.'

'Yes. You're a
bear all right,'
said Tom,
coming up. 'I
hear you've
come to live with us. Well, I'll show
you your place in the toy-cupboard –
right at the back there, look.'

'I don't like being at the back, it's
too dark,' said the little bear. 'I'll be at
the front here, by this big brick-box.'

'Oh, no you won't. That's *my*
place when I want to sit in the toy-
cupboard,' said Amelia Jane. 'And let
me tell you this, small bear – if you
live with us you'll have to take on lots

of little bits of work. We all do. You'll
have to wind up the clockwork clown
when he runs down, you'll have to
clean the dolls'-house windows, and
you'll have to help the engine-driver
polish his big red train.'

'Dear me, I don't think I want to
do any of those things,' said the bear.
'I'm lazy. I don't like working.'

'Well, you'll just have to,' said
Amelia Jane. 'Otherwise you won't get
any of the biscuit crumbs that the
children drop on the floor, you won't
get any of the sweets in the toy sweet-
shop – and we're allowed some every
week – and you won't come to any
parties. So there.'

'Pooh!' said the bear and stalked off
to pick up some beads out of the bead-
box and thread himself a necklace.

'He's vain as well as lazy,' said Tom in disgust. 'Hey, bear – what's your name? Or are you too lazy to have one?'

'My name is Sidney Gordon Eustace,' said the bear, haughtily. 'And please remember that I don't like being called Sid.'

'Sid!' yelled all the toys at once, and the bear looked furious. He turned his head away, and went on threading the beads.

'Sidney Gordon Eustace!' said the clown, with a laugh. 'I guess he gave himself those names. No sensible child would ever call a teddy bear that. Huh!'

The bear was not much use in the playroom. He just would *not* do any of the jobs there at all. He went

surprisingly deaf when anyone called
to him to come and clean or polish or
sweep. He would pretend to be asleep,
or just walk about humming a little
tune as if nobody was calling his
name at all. It was most annoying.

'Sidney! Come and shake the mats
for the dolls'-house dolls!' Tom called.
No answer from Sidney at all.

'SIDNEY! Come here! You're not
as deaf as all that!'

The bear never even turned his
head.

'Hey, Sidney Gordon Eustace –
come and do your jobs!' yelled Tom.
'SID, SID, SID!'

No answer. 'All right!' shouted
Tom, angrily. 'You shan't have that
nice big crumb of chocolate biscuit we
found under the table this morning.'

It was always the same whenever there was a job to be done. 'Sidney, come here!' But Sidney never came. He never did one single thing for any of the toys.

'What are we going to do about him?' said the big teddy bear. 'Amelia Jane – can't you think of a good idea?'

'Oh, yes,' said Amelia at once. 'I know what we'll do. We'll get Sidney-the-mouse to come and do the things that Sidney-the-bear should do – and he shall have all the crumbs and titbits that the bear should have. He won't like that – a little house-mouse getting all his treats!'

'Dear me – is the house-mouse's name Sidney, too?' said Tom in surprise. 'I never knew that before.

When we want him we usually go to
his hole and shout "Mouse" and he
comes.'

'Well, I'll go and shout "Sidney",'
said Amelia Jane, 'and you'll see –
he'll come!' So she went to the little
hole at the bottom of the wall near the
bookcase and shouted down it.

'Sidney! Sid-Sid-Sidney! We want
you!'

The little bear, of course, didn't
turn round – *he* wasn't going to come
when his name was called. But
someone very small came scampering
up the passage to the hole-entrance. It
was the tiny brown house-mouse, with
bright black eyes and twitching
whiskers.

'Ah, Sidney,' said Amelia Jane.
'Will you just come and shake the

mats in the dolls' house, please? They
are very dusty. We'll give you a big
chocolate biscuit crumb and a drink
of lemonade out of the little teapot if
you will.'

'Can I drink out of the spout?' said
the tiny mouse, pleased. 'I like
drinking out of the spout.'

'Yes, of course,' said Amelia Jane.

The little mouse set about shaking
the mats vigorously, and the job was
soon done.

'Isn't Sidney wonderful?' said
Amelia in a loud voice to the others.
'Sidney-the-mouse, I mean, of course,

not silly Sidney-the-bear. He wouldn't
have the strength to shake mats like
that, poor thing. Sidney, here's the
chocolate biscuit crumb and there's
the teapot full of lemonade.'

Sidney the bear didn't like this at
all. Fancy making a fuss of a silly
little mouse, and giving him treats
like that. He would very much have
liked the crumb and the lemonade
himself. He pressed himself in the
middle and growled furiously when
the mouse had gone.

'Don't have that mouse here
again,' he said. 'I don't like hearing
somebody else being called Sidney.
Anyway, I don't believe his name *is*
Sidney. It's not a name for a mouse.'

'Well, for all you know, his name
might be Sidney Gordon Eustace just

like yours,' said Amelia Jane at once.

'Pooh! Whoever heard of a mouse having a grand name like that?' said the bear.

'Well, next time you won't do a job, we'll call all three names down the hole,' said Amelia, 'and see if the little mouse will answer to them!'

Next night there was going to be a party. Everyone had to help to get ready for it. Amelia Jane called to the little bear.

'Sidney! Come and set the tables for the party. Sidney, do you hear me?'

Sidney did, but he pretended not to, of course. Set party tables! Not he! So he went deaf again, and didn't even turn his head.

'Sidney Gordon Eustace, do as

you're told or you won't come to the party,' bawled the big teddy bear in a fine old rage.

The little bear didn't answer. Amelia Jane gave a sudden grin.

'Never mind,' she said. 'We'll get Sidney Gordon Eustace, the little mouse, to come and set the tables. He does them beautifully and never breaks a thing. He can come to the party afterwards then. I'll call him.'

The little bear turned his head. 'He won't answer to *that* name, you know he won't!' he said, scornfully. 'Call away! No mouse ever had a name as grand as mine.'

Amelia Jane went to the mouse-hole and called down it.

'Sidney Gordon Eustace, are you there?' she called. 'If you are at home, come up and help us. Sidney Gordon Eustace, are you there?'

And at once there came the pattering of tiny feet, and with a loud squeak the little mouse peeped out of his hole, his whiskers quivering.

'Ah – you are at home,' said Amelia. 'Well, dear little Sidney, will you set the tables for us? We're going to have a party.'

The mouse was delighted. He was soon at work, and in a short while the four tables were set with tiny table-cloths and china. Then he went to help the dolls'-house dolls to cut sandwiches. The bear watched all this out of the corner of his eye. He was quite amazed that the mouse had come when he was called Sidney Gordon Eustace – goodness, fancy a little mouse owning a name like that!

He was very cross when he saw
that the mouse was going to the
party. Amelia Jane found
him a red ribbon to tie
round his neck and
one for his
long tail. He
was given a place at the
biggest table, and
everyone made a fuss of him.

'Good little Sidney! You do work
well! Whatever should we do without
you? What will you have to eat?'

The mouse ate a lot. *Much* too
much, the little bear thought. He
didn't go to the party. He hadn't been
asked and he didn't quite like to go
because there was no chair for him
and no plate. But, oh, all those nice

things to eat! *Why* hadn't he been sensible and gone to set the tables?

'Goodnight, Sidney Gordon Eustace,' said Amelia to the delighted mouse. 'We've loved having you.'

Now, after this kind of thing had happened three or four times the bear got tired of it.

He hated hearing people yell for 'Sidney, Sidney!' down the mouse-hole, or to hear the mouse addressed as Sidney Gordon Eustace. It was really too bad. Also, the mouse was getting all the titbits and the treats. The bear didn't like that either.

So the next time that there was a job to be done the bear decided to do it. He suddenly heard Tom say 'Hallo! The big red engine is very smeary. It wants a polish again. I'll go and call Sidney.'

Tom went to the mouse-hole and began to call down it. 'Sidney, Sidney, Sidney!'

But before the mouse could answer, Sidney the bear rushed up to Tom. 'Yes! Did you call me? What do you want me to do?'

'Dear me – you're not as deaf as usual!' said Tom, surprised. 'Well, go and polish the red engine, then. You can have a sweet out of the toy sweet shop if you do it properly.'

Sidney did do it properly. Tom came and looked at the engine and so did Amelia Jane. 'Very nice,' said Amelia. 'Give him a big sweet, Tom.'

The bear was pleased. Aha! He had done the mouse out of a job. The toys had been pleased with him, and

the sweet was delicious.

And after that, dear me, you
should have seen Sidney the bear rush
up whenever his name was called.
'Yes, yes – here I am. What do you
want me to do?'

Very soon the little mouse was not
called up from the hole any more, and
Sidney the bear worked hard and was
friendly and sensible. The toys began
to like him, and Sidney liked them too.

But one thing puzzled Tom and the big teddy bear, and they asked Amelia Jane about it.

'Amelia Jane – HOW did you know that the mouse's name was Sidney Gordon Eustace?'

'It isn't,' said Amelia with a grin.

'But it must be,' said Tom. 'He always came when you called him by it.'

'I know – but he'd come if you called *any* name down his hole,' said Amelia. 'Go and call what name you like – he'll come! It's the calling he answers, not the name! He doesn't even know what names are!'

'Good gracious!' said Tom and the bear, and they went to the mouse-hole.

'William!' called Tom, and up

came the mouse. He was given a
crumb and went down again.

'Polly-Wolly-Doodle!' shouted the
big bear, and up came the mouse for
another crumb.

'Boot-polish!' shouted Tom, and
up came the mouse.

'Tomato soup!' cried the big bear.

And it didn't matter what name was yelled down the hole, the mouse always came up. He came because he heard a loud shout, that was all. Amelia Jane went off into fits of laughter when the mouse came up at different calls. 'Penny stamp! Cough-drop! Sid-Sid-Sid! Dickory-Dock! Rub-a-dub-dub!'

The mouse's nose appeared at the hole each time. How the toys laughed – all except Sidney the bear!

He didn't laugh. He felt very silly indeed. Oh, dear – what a trick Amelia Jane had played on him! But suddenly he began to laugh, too. 'It's funny,' he cried. 'It's funny!'

It certainly was. Amelia *would* think of a good idea like that, wouldn't she?

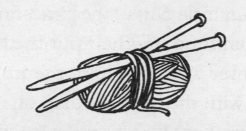

Amelia Jane is Very Busy

One day Amelia Jane sat very still in her little chair, and watched somebody knitting in the playroom. It was little Miss Jones, who came to help with the children's clothes. She was knitting a jersey for the biggest boy.

'Click-click-clickety-click!' Her knitting needles flashed in and out all day long, and Amelia Jane watched and watched.

When little Miss Jones had finished all the knitting and had put the balls of left-over wool neatly in the work-basket with the long needles, she left the playroom to go home.

As soon as she had gone Amelia Jane ran to the work-basket. She took up two needles and a ball of wool and went to sit on the rug by herself, leaning against the table-leg.

'I can knit,' she told the toys. 'I know how to. I watched Miss Jones all day long. You go like this – and like that – and see,

the knitting comes!'

The toys watched her. They thought Amelia Jane was very clever. Click-click-clickity-click – why, her needles went as fast as Miss Jones' needles!

'What are you making?' asked the sailor doll.

'Nothing. I'm just knitting,' said Amelia.

'But you must be knitting *something*,' said the clockwork mouse. 'You can't just *knit*.'

'It's a waste of wool not to make something when you knit,' said the teddy bear. 'Can't you make me a jersey?'

'No. It would take me ages to knit a jersey to go over your fat little tummy,' said Amelia Jane.

'Don't be rude,' said the bear, offended. 'If *you* kept a growl in your tummy, you'd be fat, too. Grrr!'

'Couldn't you knit me a bonnet?' said the baby doll. 'I could do with a new one.'

'No, I couldn't. You've got three already,' said Amelia Jane. 'For goodness' sake go away and let me *knit*! I tell you, I'm not making anything at all, I'm just knitting.'

The baby doll sat down by her and took off her hair-ribbon to smooth it out. She was very particular about her ribbons. She put it down beside her, and began to comb out her hair with a little comb.

'Go away,' said Amelia. 'I don't like people who comb hair all over me.'

76

'Well, you can just put up with it,' said the baby doll, crossly. 'I can sit where I like.'

Amelia Jane didn't say anything – but when the baby doll looked for her hair-ribbon it had gone!

'You've taken it!' she said to Amelia. 'You mean thing. Give it back.'

'She can't. She's knitted it with the wool!' said Tom, pointing. And sure enough that bad Amelia Jane had taken the ribbon and knitted it – and there was the ribbon, right in the very middle of the knitting.

'I can't take it out,' said Amelia. 'It would spoil my beautiful knitting. You'll have to do without your ribbon now. It's your own fault.'

The baby doll went off, crying.

'Cry-baby!' said Amelia Jane, and went on knitting.

'Your knitting is nothing but a long, long scarf, very narrow,' said the bear. 'It's silly knitting. Nobody would wear a scarf like that.'

'Nobody's going to,' said Amelia Jane. 'I wish you would stop bothering me. Can't I knit if I want to?'

'The click-click noise makes me cross,' said the sailor doll.

'It doesn't take much to make you cross,' said Amelia. 'Clockwork mouse, what do *you* want? Don't you dare to nibble my wool!'

'I just want to watch you knit,' said the mouse, and he sat down close by. And will you believe it, that rascally Amelia Jane knitted his long tail into her knitting! The little mouse

suddenly found himself pulled
towards Amelia's knitting, and saw
his tail there!

Goodness, what a to-do there was!
The bear was very angry. 'You can't
do things like this, Amelia!' he said.

'I can,' she said. 'And I have. The
mouse can't have his tail back. It
belongs to my knitting now.'

But the sailor doll made her undo

the tail because the clockwork mouse was so upset.

'He can't hang on to your knitting by his tail,' he told Amelia Jane.

'You're very unkind and very silly. Just *look* at the enormous length of knitting you have done – all for nothing, too!'

The next thing he knew was that Amelia had pulled out his bootlaces and had knitted those, too! She would not give them back, either, and the sailor doll stamped round the nursery in a rage, his boots slipping off his feet every minute!

'She'll have to fall asleep sometime soon,' whispered the teddy bear to the toy soldier. 'Then we'll pay her out for all this!'

So they waited till her needles

worked more and more slowly –
clickity-click, clickity-click – click –
click – click – click – and then they
stopped. Amelia Jane was fast asleep!

The toys crept up to her. They
took up the long, long strip of
knitting. They wound it all round
Amelia Jane and the table-leg she was
leaning against – round and round
and round and round!

'Now she's all tied up in her own
knitting!' said Tom,
pleased. 'And the more
she knits, the more tied

up she will get.'

Amelia Jane woke up merry and bright. She picked up her knitting needles and started off again – clickity-click, clickity-click!

But soon she found that she was bound tightly to the table-leg, and the more she pulled at her knitting, the tighter it became. She tried to stand up – but she couldn't.

'Oh! Oh! I've knitted myself to the table-leg!' she cried. 'Toys, help me!'

'Certainly *not*,' said the clockwork clown with a squeal of delight. 'Go on knitting. You'll soon be right in the middle of it and we shan't see you again! Knit hard, Amelia, knit hard!'

Amelia Jane didn't. She stopped. She tugged at the knitting to try to free herself but she couldn't. And dear

me, how scared she got when she saw
how the knitting was wound round
and round and round herself and the
table-leg!

'Undo me!' she begged the baby
doll.

'I will if you knit me a new
bonnet,' said the doll.

'Undo me!' Amelia Jane begged
the bear.

'I will if you knit me a jersey and
don't say anything about my fat little
tummy,' said the bear.

'And you can knit me a red
waistcoat,' said Tom.

'And me a new vest,' said the sailor
doll.

'All right,' said Amelia. 'You're
mean, all of you. But I'll knit what
you want – and I hope nothing fits,

so there!'

Well, they undid Amelia Jane from the table-leg, and then they helped her to pull undone all the long, long piece of knitting.

Out came the sailor's bootlaces and the baby doll's ribbon!

And then she had to set to work to keep her promises. She has made the bear a tight little red jersey.

'You'll never be able to get it off

again, once you've got it on,' Tom told him, so the poor bear can't make up his mind whether to wear it or not.

Amelia has made the sailor a

new vest, but as it reaches down to his feet he doesn't quite know what to do with it!

As for Tom's waistcoat, it's got three armholes instead of two! 'Use one for a leg!' said Amelia with a giggle. But how can he do that?

And now Amelia is knitting the bonnet for the baby doll, but as it is already big enough to go all round the teddy bear's middle, I expect she will have to use it for a shawl!

Can't you be sensible, Amelia Jane – just for once? Tie her up to the table-leg again, toys! She's just too bad for words.

Oh, Bother Amelia Jane!

'What are you doing, Amelia Jane?' asked the sailor doll. 'What do you want that water for?'

'I'm going to paint,' said Amelia. 'See, I've found a paint-box in the toy-cupboard. I know how to paint because I've watched the children.'

'How do you paint?' asked the sailor doll.

Amelia Jane dipped her paint-brush into the water and then rubbed it on one of the little squares of colour in the paint-box.

'I paint like this!' she said with a giggle and splashed a big stripe of green all across the sailor doll's face!

He was very angry. He went off to tell the other toys. 'She's in one of her silly moods again,' he said to Tom. 'We'd better look out!'

Amelia Jane painted hard all the morning. At first she painted pictures on a piece of paper. Then she looked round for something better to do with her paints.

'The dolls' house! I'll paint monkeys climbing up the wall,' she said. 'The little dolls have gone out for a walk – they'll be surprised when they come back!'

So she painted little brown monkeys all the way up the front walls of the pretty little dolls' house – they did look peculiar!

The dolls'-house dolls screamed when they came back. 'Look! What's that on the walls? Monkeys! Are they real? Oh, what's happened to our dear little house?'

'You be careful in case there are

monkeys inside it too!' said Amelia Jane, and not one of the tiny dolls dared to go in at their front door!

Then she saw the little wooden train standing by itself in a corner of the room. The engine-driver had gone to talk to the teddy bear, so he wasn't there. Amelia Jane took her pot of water and paint-box – and do you know what she did? She painted rows of silly faces all round the engine and its trucks!

'Look! What's happened? Where did these dreadful faces come from?' cried the engine-driver when he saw them. 'My beautiful train! Everyone will laugh at me when I drive it.'

'You'd better get a cloth and rub all the faces off,' said Tom. 'Bother Amelia Jane! I'll help you,

Engine-driver.'

So they spent a long, long time trying to get the faces off the engine and the train. They were very hot and tired by the end of it.

'I'd be much obliged if you would go and give Amelia Jane a good telling-off from me,' said the engine-driver. 'I'm too small to do it myself.'

'With pleasure,' said Tom and he went up to Amelia Jane, and gave her a good scolding. She was very angry – and you can guess what she did! She painted his hat white when he was asleep!

It did look strange.

He was very much upset. All the toys stood round him and giggled.

'What happened?' said the teddy bear. 'Your hat's all white, Tom!'

Tom had to climb up to the little wash-basin, turn on a tap, put the plug in, and try to wash the white off his hat. He managed to get himself wet all over, and the white ran down his jacket and trousers.

So then he had to sit in front of the fire, and when his jacket dried it shrank and was so tight that he could hardly breathe. He was very, very cross with Amelia Jane!

She painted the clockwork mouse's tail a bright red, and he thought it was a worm running after him. He raced away, squealing, 'I can't get away from that red worm; it follows me, it follows me!' The toys couldn't help laughing.

'It's only your tail. Don't be afraid of your own tail,' said the bear. 'Go and climb up to the bookshelf, where the bowl of goldfish is. Sit on the edge and dip your tail into the water. The red will run off and you will be all right again.'

'Yes, you do that,' said Amelia Jane, with a grin. *She* knew what would happen, but the others didn't! The clockwork mouse got up on to the bookcase, and went to the goldfish bowl. He sat on the edge and dipped his red tail into the water.

The goldfish were very excited. 'A worm! A lovely long red worm!' they bubbled to one another. 'Quick, catch it and eat it!'

And they swam to the little red tail and snapped at it. Goodness – the mouse almost fell backwards into the water! 'Don't! Don't! That's

my tail!' he squealed.

He only just managed to get it out of the bowl before it was nibbled off. He raced down to the floor, tumbling over and over when he got there.

Amelia Jane laughed and laughed. The clockwork mouse cried bitterly. 'I wish *you* had a tail!' he said to Amelia Jane. 'I'd come and nibble it, then you'd know how it felt!'

Now the next night, a small mouse, a real one this time, came running out of a hole in the playroom wall with a little note in his mouth. It was from the toys in the next house.

'I say!' said the clockwork clown, reading the note. 'The toys next door are giving a fancy dress party! What fun! It's the night after next. Well, *I* shall go as a pirate!'

'I shall go as one of the bears in the story of The Three Bears,' said the teddy bear.

'And I shall make myself a red cloak and hood and go as Red Riding Hood,' said the tiny doll in the corner of the toy-cupboard.

'I shall go as a queen,' said Amelia Jane, grandly. 'I can easily make myself a crown, and there's a beautiful dress laid away in a box in one of the drawers over there. I can make a cloak, and I have got a very pretty necklace that came out of a cracker.'

Well, Amelia Jane worked very hard indeed at making the lovely cloak. It was royal purple and she sewed tiny silver beads all over it, from the bead box. She tried on her crown – how lovely she looked! She put on the necklace.

'Don't I look beautiful?' she said to the other toys. 'I shall win the first prize for the fancy dress. I know I shall!'

Tom thought she probably would. 'You don't deserve to,' he said. 'You've been unkind. The clockwork mouse is still upset because the red hasn't properly come off his tail.'

'Pooh!' said Amelia Jane. 'You wait till I get the paint-box out again. I'll do MUCH worse things than that!'

That made the toys very angry. The bear decided to take the paint-box and hide it when Amelia wasn't looking. It was quite easy to do that because she was so tired that night with her hard work sewing on the silver beads that she fell asleep!

'Look at her – fast asleep!' said Tom. 'She doesn't *deserve* to win the first prize at the party. But she will!'

'She won't,' said the bear, suddenly. 'I've got an idea, Tom. Listen – *I* can paint just as well as Amelia Jane can. And I'm going to paint her face in all kinds of stripes and dots while she's asleep! It'll be red and blue and green and yellow!'

The toys stood and giggled as the bear took the paint-brush, dipped it into the little pot of water, and began to paint Amelia's sleeping face. Goodness, he did it well! Stripes of red and green, dots of blue and yellow, crosses of black and brown.

Oh dear – what a terrifying sight Amelia Jane looked!

'But she'll see herself in the mirror, won't she?' said the clockwork mouse.

'No, because she would have to climb up on the bookcase, and stand there to see herself in the mirror on the wall,' said the bear. 'And she won't do that when she's wearing a cloak. She couldn't climb in that.'

Well, when Amelia Jane woke up,

she didn't know anything about her
painted face, of course. All the toys
put on fancy dresses for the party –
and Amelia Jane couldn't *think* why
they giggled every time they looked at
her. In fact the
clockwork
mouse laughed
so much that his
key fell out.

Amelia walked up and down,
wearing her crown and necklace, with
the beautiful silk dress going 'swish-
swish-swish' all the time, and her
cloak flying out behind her, gleaming
with silver beads. She didn't know
how funny she looked, with her
painted face, all stripes and dots and
crosses!

'First prize for *me*!' she said to the

toys. 'Don't you think so?'

That made them giggle again, of course. Amelia Jane simply couldn't understand them. 'You're being very silly tonight,' she said. 'Well – I'm just going out into the passage to look at myself in the long mirror there. I don't want to climb up to the bookcase mirror in this long cloak.'

The toys had quite forgotten *that* mirror! They wondered whatever Amelia Jane would say when she saw herself. She walked out into the passage – and then she gave a loud scream.

'Oh! OH! My face! What's happened to it? Oh, you wicked bad toys, you've painted it! And I haven't time to wash it off properly. Oh, you horrid mean things.'

'We've only done to you what you did to us!' said Tom, grinning. 'You can't go to the party like that – and it serves you right!'

'I shall come! I shall! You just see!' cried Amelia Jane, and she took off her crown and necklace and began to undo her cloak. 'Yes, and I'll get first prize, too! Oh, you unkind things!'

'Well, we won't wait. It's time we set off,' said the bear. 'Goodbye, Amelia Jane. We are sorry we shan't see you at the fancy dress party.'

But all the same Amelia is going! I look like an Indian, with war-paint on my face! she thought, as she threw off her lovely dress. All right – I'll go as an Indian! Where's that little shuttle-cock with coloured feathers set round it? They will do for my hair!

She pulled out the feathers and set them round her head. Then she looked for the little wigwam tent that the bear and Tom sometimes played with. It was painted brightly.

'That will do for a cloak,' said Amelia. 'And where's that rubber axe? Ah, here it is – that shall be my tomahawk! And who shall be my enemies? The toy soldier, the bear and all the rest! Look out – I'm coming to the party after all!'

And off she went at top speed, the fiercest Indian you ever saw. What a shock the toys are going to get! I can only hope that naughty Amelia Jane doesn't win the first prize after all!

Goodbye,
Amelia Jane!

The toys played a trick on Amelia Jane the other day.

Amelia Jane was always playing tricks on all the toys in the nursery. There was no end to her mischief. If she didn't think of one thing, she thought of another.

There was the time when she collected worms in the garden and popped them all into Tom's shut umbrella. They wriggled about there and couldn't get out, poor things.

And then Amelia sent Tom out into the garden to fetch her hanky from the garden seat. It was raining, of course, so she gave him his umbrella.

'Better put this up,' she said, and he did. And out slithered all the worms, on top of his head and down his neck, as soon as he got out into the garden in the rain.

The worms fled into holes very

thankfully, but Tom got such a fright that he ran straight into the pond and got wet through.

He was very, very angry with
Amelia Jane, but she only laughed.

'You shouldn't let worms nest in
your umbrella,' she said.

Another time, Amelia took the
teapot out of the toy tea-set and
filled it with hot water from the
tap. Then she climbed up to the
roof of the
dolls' house and
poured the hot

water down the chimney.

The little dolls'-house dolls rushed out of the front door in fright, with water trickling down the stairs after them, and Amelia Jane nearly fell off the roof with laughing.

She was well scolded for that bit of mischief, but she wouldn't even say she was sorry.

The toys had a meeting about her.

'I'm tired of Amelia Jane,' said the toy soldier.

'So am I,' said the clockwork clown. 'She took my key away yesterday for about the fiftieth time.'

'Can't we get rid of her?' said the teddy bear.

'We've often tried,' said the clockwork mouse. 'But we never have.'

'I've got an idea,' said Tom, his

eyes shining brightly. 'It's a small idea at the moment – but if we talk about it, it might grow into a big one and be really good.'

'What is it?' asked the clockwork clown.

'Well – you know you can slide down the stairs on a tray, don't you?' said Tom.

Everyone nodded.

'That's my idea,' said Tom. 'It's only just that. I haven't thought any more than that.'

'It seems rather silly,' said the bear. 'Did you mean to get Amelia Jane to slide down the stairs on a tray, or what?'

'I don't know,' said Tom. 'I tell you, I hadn't thought any further than I said.'

'Ooooh!' said the clown. '*Could* we make her slide down on a tray – push her very, very hard . . . ?'

'And have the front door open so that she shot right out in a hurry,' went on the bear.

'And have the garden gate open so that she'd shoot out there, too,' said the clown.

'And then down the hill she'd go, whizz-bang, faster and faster and faster,' said the clockwork mouse, excitedly.

'And splash into the stream on her tray, and off it would go like a boat, all the way down to the sea!' finished Tom, his face beaming with excitement.

'And we'd never, never see her again, the bad, naughty doll,' said the bear.

'No, we wouldn't. We'd shout,

"Goodbye, Amelia Jane!" when she flew out of the front door, and that would be that,' said Tom. 'See what my little idea has grown to – a great big one. I thought it would!'

Well, the toys talked and talked about their idea, and got very excited about it indeed. Surely they could at last get rid of that naughty Amelia Jane!

Amelia didn't know anything about all this, of course. She was out in the garden collecting a few more worms to play another trick. Tom had time to get out the big tin tray from its corner and rub soap underneath it to make it more slippery.

'We'll play our trick when everyone is out tomorrow,' he decided. 'If I stand on a chair in the hall I can open the front door all right. Now, don't say a word about our plan, any of you!'

The next afternoon the house was very quiet because everyone had gone out. Tom took the tin tray and banged hard on it. 'Boom, diddy-boom!'

'Stop that noise,' said Amelia Jane, crossly. 'I want to have a snooze.'

'All right. Have one,' said Tom. 'We are all going to the top of the stairs to play at sliding down on this tea-tray. We'll have a lovely time – and we don't want *you*, Amelia Jane!'

Well, that was quite enough to make Amelia want to come, of course! 'I'm coming, too,' she said. 'And I guess I'll go faster down the stairs than any of you!'

Off they all went to the top of the stairs. Tom ran down, got a chair, stood on it, and opened the front door. He ran back and had his turn at sliding down. The tray went down to the bottom, bumpity-bumpity-bump, slid a little way down the hall and stopped. Aha! If they all pushed hard when Amelia Jane had her turn, it would most certainly fly out of the door, down the path, out of the gate and away down the hill to the stream at the bottom!

'I want my turn, I want mine!' shouted Amelia, and she got on to the tray. She held tight – and the toy soldier, the bear, the clockwork clown, the mouse and another doll all pushed as hard as ever they could.

Whoooooosh! You should have

seen that tray fly down the stairs at top speed! Amelia's breath was quite taken away. Her hair and her dress flew out behind her, and she stared in fright. This was a much faster journey than she had imagined!

Down to the bottom of the stairs – along the hall at top speed – out of the open door – down the slippery front path – out of the open gate – and whoooooosh – down the steep hill that led to the stream!

'Goodbye, Amelia Jane!' shouted the toys. 'Goodbye, goodbye!'

'She's gone,' said the bear, after a pause. 'Really gone. She'll never tease us again.'

'Never,' said Tom, pleased. 'She's played her last trick on us.'

'She deserved to be shot off like

that,'
said the
clown. 'Now
let's play at sliding
trays downstairs all by
ourselves.'

They played for quite a long time. Then they went back to the nursery to have a drink of water.

'I just hope Amelia Jane didn't tip off the tray going down the hill, and hurt herself,' said the bear, suddenly.

'And I just hope she didn't fall into the stream and get drowned,' said the clown.

'It seems a bit funny without her,' said the mouse. 'Er – you don't suppose we were dreadfully unkind, do you?'

'Not a bit,' said Tom. 'She deserved to be sent off like that.'

'But you wouldn't want her to hurt herself, would you?' said the bear, solemnly. 'You know – I keep on and on thinking what would happen if she tipped off the tray going down-hill – suppose she fell under a bus – or . . .'

The clockwork mouse gave a squeal of fright. 'Don't say things like that. They frighten me. You make me feel as if I want Amelia Jane back.'

'Perhaps she wasn't as bad as she seemed,' said the bear. 'You know – I don't feel very nice about playing that trick on her now. I feel sort of

114

uncomfortable.'

'Pooh!' said Tom, but he didn't say any more.

Well, what *had* happened to Amelia Jane? She had slid out into the front garden and out of the gate, and down the hill at top speed. She was very frightened indeed. Why had the toys shouted goodbye? Was it a trick they had played on her to get rid of her? Amelia Jane wailed aloud as she shot down the hill. Oh dear, oh dear, had she been so dreadful that the toys wanted to get rid of her like that?

'I'm going straight into the stream!' she squealed, and splash, into the water she went. She clung to the tray. It didn't sink, but bobbed on the surface, with a very wet Amelia

Jane clinging on top. Down the stream she went, bobbing on the waves.

She floated for a very long way. Then the tray bumped into the bank, stuck into some weeds and stopped. Amelia thankfully crawled off on to the land. She was wet and cold and tired. She could see a dog not far off and she was frightened of him.

Where could she hide? What was that lying on the grass over there? A bicycle! It had a basket behind the saddle, and Amelia Jane staggered off to it. She squeezed into the basket, and stuffed an old bit of newspaper over herself. Now, perhaps, nobody, not even the dog, would see her.

She fell asleep and dreamed of the toys. She dreamt that they were all cross with her, and she cried in her sleep.

'Don't be cross with me. I'll be good, I'll be good.'

Then she woke up – and dear me, she was wobbling from side to side in the basket. Somebody had picked up the bicycle, mounted it, and was now riding away down the river path – with Amelia Jane tucked into the basket at the back.

Oh, dear! thought Amelia, in a panic. 'Now where am I going? I'm miles and miles away from home – and from all the toys. I wish I was back again. Wouldn't I be good if I could only get back to the nursery! But the toys wouldn't be pleased to see me at all. They'd turn me out again.'

On she went and on. Miles and miles it seemed to Amelia Jane, and she grew cramped and cold in the basket. And then, at last, the rider stopped and jumped off.

He flung his bicycle against something, and walked off, whistling.

Amelia Jane peeped out. The bicycle was against a wall near a back door. She crawled out of the basket, and almost fell to the ground. She ran to the door. If only she could get into a house, she could hide.

In she went, and somebody jumped in surprise as the big doll ran past. Amelia tore into the hall and up the stairs. She almost fell inside a room, and stopped there, panting in fright.

And will you believe it, she was

back in the nursery again – and there were all the toys she knew, staring at her in amazement – the toy soldier, the bear, the clown, the mouse and everyone!

She had come all the way home in the basket of the bicycle belonging to one of the children! He had gone to the river that day, and then had cycled all the way back – and Amelia Jane was in his basket. What a very, very peculiar thing!

'You said goodbye to me – but here I am again,' said Amelia, in a funny, shaky sort of voice. 'It seems as if you c-c-c-can't get rid of me!'

She burst into tears – and then everyone ran to comfort her. She was patted and fussed, and even Tom kept saying he was glad to see her back.

'Oh, dear – this is all so nice,' said Amelia at last. 'I won't be mischievous again, toys. I won't play tricks any more. I'll be just as good as gold!'

'We don't believe you,' said Tom. 'But never mind – we're glad to have you back, you bad, naughty doll. We never *really* want to say goodbye to you, Amelia Jane!'

I don't either. What about you?

She's big! She's bad!

She's the terror of the toy cupboard... and she's back!

More adventures from Amelia Jane.

EGMONT